My Pet Slime

Cosmo to the Rescue

Courtney Sheinmel
Illustrated by Renée Kurilla

Andrews McMeel
PUBLISHING®

My Pet Slime:
Cosmo to the Rescue

Andrews McMeel Publishing
a division of Andrews McMeel Universal
1130 Walnut Street, Kansas City, Missouri 64106

www.andrewsmcmeel.com

Epic! Creations, Inc.
702 Marshall Street, Suite 280,
Redwood City, California 94063

www.getepic.com

20 21 22 23 24 SDB 10 9 8 7 6 5 4 3 2 1

Paperback ISBN: 978-1-5248-6294-7
Hardback ISBN: 978-1-5248-5573-4

Library of Congress Control Number: 2019951258

Design by Ariana Abud and Wendy Gable

Made by:
King Yip (Dongguan) Printing & Packaging Factory Ltd.
Address and location of production:
Daning Administrative District, Humen Town
Dongguan Guangdong, China 523930
1st Printing — 6/1/20

ATTENTION: SCHOOLS AND BUSINESSES
Andrews McMeel books are available at quantity
discounts with bulk purchase for educational, business,
or sales promotional use. For information, please
e-mail the Andrews McMeel Publishing Special Sales
Department: specialsales@amuniversal.com

Wow and Pow

At the end of each day, my dad likes to ask me what my wow and pow were.

The wow means the best part of your day.

The pow means the worst part.

Want some examples? Well...

If you had a mostly bad day because you dropped your lunch in the mud on the way to school, and your teacher made you feel bad in front of the whole class because you forgot to do your spelling homework, and it was still raining on the way home, your wow can be something small, like at least your umbrella didn't break.

Or if you had a mostly good day because the sun was shining, and it was your birthday, and you got all the presents you wished for, plus the world's most delicious cake, your pow can be something as teeny tiny as getting a paper cut from the wrapping paper.

Sometimes it's hard to decide what my wows and pows are, and I have to think really hard to come up with something.

But today I didn't have to think hard at all.

My wow was: I have a new pet!

I made him myself, out of slime.

I know, I know—a slime pet doesn't sound like a real pet. But Cosmo *is* real. That's his name, by the way: Cosmo. He's as friendly as a hamster, and he can do tricks like a dog. But mostly he likes to cuddle with me.

I've never had a pet before, and having Cosmo is the wowest wow I've ever had.

But my pow was: My grandma is missing.

My parents are pretending that it's not a big deal. They say Grandma Sadie takes mysterious trips all the time without telling us where she's going.

That part is true. Grandma works at AstroBlast Explorers, and her job is to go out and explore space. She's not allowed to talk about it that much.

But her boss at AstroBlast Explorers always knows where she is, even if she doesn't tell us.

Except not this time. Her boss called

Mom and said that Grandma Sadie didn't show up to work. Grandma's boss doesn't know where she is. NO ONE knows where she is.

I know my parents are scared, even if they won't admit it. I'm scared, too. It's the powest pow I've ever had.

Sometimes, when your pow is really bad, it's hard to be excited about your wow, no matter how big of a wow it is.

That's how I was feeling. I loved Cosmo so much, but he couldn't distract me from being worried about Grandma Sadie.

Mom and Dad told me it was time for bed. They each came in to say goodnight. Mom rubbed my back, which is what she does when I'm having trouble falling asleep. I closed my eyes and breathed a little bit deeper, so she'd think I was sleeping. She gave me a kiss on the forehead and walked out the door.

I heard the click of the door closing and opened my eyes. "Cosmo?" I said.

He gurgled from under my bed, and I reached down to pick him up.

Mom and Dad think Cosmo is just a blob of slime and not a real pet. That's because he comes alive only for me, and not for anyone else.

Oh, except for Claire. She's the most popular kid in my class at school. For some reason, Cosmo comes alive for her, too. I wanted to figure out why. But I was too busy worrying about Grandma Sadie to think about it.

"Grandma Sadie is the reason you're here," I told Cosmo. "Did you know that?"

Cosmo gurgled. Did that mean yes or no? I wasn't sure. So I decided to explain it to him: "Yesterday I made slime in my room. I'm not allowed to make slime in my room...but that's not the important part of this story. What's important is that I shaped my slime into something that looked like a pet. It was the size of a kitten, but rounder, with big eyes, a teeny mouth, and arms just long enough to give hugs. That probably sounds familiar, because I was making you!"

I squeezed Cosmo closer, and he hugged me back.

"Oh, you're the coziest pet ever," I said. "But at first, I didn't think you were a real pet because, well, slime isn't usually alive. Then Grandma Sadie came over for dinner. She'd been on a trip to a secret destination in space, and she brought me back a present."

Cosmo gurgled. I'm pretty sure he was asking, "What was the present?"

"I'll tell you what it was," I said.

"It was space dust! The thing about space dust is that it looks a lot like regular dust. But regular dust isn't that special, so at first, I wasn't excited. But when I got into bed, I heard a strange sound coming from the bottle of space dust. I got up to check things out. That's when I noticed that the dust had started glowing. I opened the bottle. The dust flew out and landed on *you*. You were just a blob back then, but you sparkled and turned alive. So you see, Cosmo, Grandma didn't really give me dust as a present. She gave me a new best friend."

Cosmo and I cuddled some more. It felt really cozy. I closed my eyes and tried to go to sleep, but it was no use.

"I'm really worried about Grandma Sadie," I said, opening my eyes again. "I have to do something about it. Will you help me?"

Cosmo gurgled, and I knew he meant yes.

Dear Piper MacLane

The problem was, I didn't know what Cosmo or I could do about Grandma Sadie. I didn't know where she was, and I didn't know how to find her. All I had was her email address.

I wrote her a "thank you for the space

dust" email last night, and I already checked to see if she wrote back. She didn't.

"Let's check my email again," I told Cosmo. "Maybe she wrote back since the last time I looked. If she hasn't, we'll send another email. Do you think that's a good idea?"

Cosmo nodded his head.

"Did you just nod?!" I cried. "Oh, wow, Cosmo! You've never nodded before. That's a brand-new trick. I'm so proud of you! Can you shake your head, too?"

Cosmo nodded.

"No, boy," I said. "That's another nod, not a shake."

But then I realized that I probably
needed to ask him a *no*-answer question
to get a shake. Hmm...

"Are Brussels sprouts your favorite
food?" I asked.

Cosmo shook his head.

"Me neither," I said. "Good boy! But enough tricks for now. We have an email to write. Let's go to Dad's office."

Dad's office is here, in our house. That's where he writes his books. I held Cosmo in my arms as I crept down the hall. The door to Mom and Dad's bedroom was mostly closed, but not all the way. I knew we had to be extra careful. I held my finger to my lips so Cosmo would know not to make a sound—not even a single gurgle.

I tiptoed closer and closer. I could hear Mom and Dad's voices on the other side of the door.

"I'm sure this is all a misunderstanding, Erin," Dad said. Erin is my mom's name. "By tomorrow, or maybe the day after, Sadie will let everyone know where she is, and we'll all laugh about how worried we were."

"I hope so, Tom," Mom said. Tom is my dad's name. "Because I'm certainly *not* laughing now."

See? I knew they were scared, too.

I put Cosmo on my shoulder and got down on my hands and knees to crawl past the door. That way, Mom and Dad wouldn't even see my shadow. One turn at the end of the hall and we were at Dad's office. I closed the door softly behind me and raced to the computer.

Oops. I forgot to turn on the light! I needed light to be able to see the keyboard. I was about to head back to flip the switch, but before I could, Cosmo blinked and started to glow. Seconds later, he was as bright as a lightbulb.

"Whoa, Cosmo!" I said. "That trick is amazing. Way better than nodding or shaking your head, or even learning to sit or fetch!"

He gurgled, and I could tell he was proud of himself. He stayed right there on the desk, the cutest light in the whole world, while I logged into my

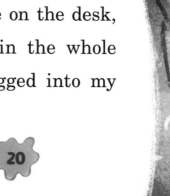

email account. I pressed enter and held my breath.

Please let there be an email from Grandma, I thought. *Please, please, please.*

My email showed that I had one new message. It had to be from Grandma. It just *had* to be.

But when I clicked on my inbox, the name of the sender was someone I'd never heard of before. Someone named MaLa.

Capital M, lowercase a, capital L, lowercase a.

A weird name, and no last name. My heart thumped as I read what she had written.

Dear Piper Maclane,

This email will disappear within five minutes of being opened, so you better read fast.

You have something we want, and we have something you want. Or should we say, we have someone you want.

If you want to see your grandmother again, you need to bury the bottle of space dust in the window box outside your bedroom. Do this before the sun comes up tomorrow morning. We'll take care of the rest.

Don't tell anyone about this email.

Sincerely,

MaLa

"Cosmo!" I cried. "Grandma Sadie's been kidnapped!"

Planting Dust

Dad's office door swung open, and the Cosmo-light went dark.

"Piper!" Dad said. "What are you doing in here?"

He flicked on the light switch and stepped toward me—and toward the computer screen. But MaLa had said not to tell anyone. What would happen to Grandma if Dad saw the email?

"No, Dad!" I cried. "You can't come in here!"

"Of course I can," Dad said. "It's *my* office. But you shouldn't be in here—not this late, not without my permission, and not with slime."

Poor Cosmo. He was just a nonglowing slime blob again.

"Didn't Mom have a conversation with you about the dos and don'ts of slime last night?" Dad asked.

"She said I wasn't allowed to make slime by myself in my room," I said.

"Right," Dad said. "And you're also not allowed to have it that close to my computer. I don't want the keyboard to get sticky. Now, what are you hiding?"

"Nothing," I lied, crossing my fingers under the desk.

Dad took one more step and looked at the computer screen. My heart began to pound. But the second that he got close enough to see the screen, the email from MaLa disappeared.

I didn't think it would really happen. How did it do that? Was it magic?

My other, old emails were still up on the screen.

"You're checking your email?" Dad asked.

I nodded.

"Oh, Piper," he said. "I know you're worried about Grandma Sadie and want to hear from her."

I nodded again. That was true. "She didn't write me back yet," I said.

"Don't you worry," Dad said. "Grandma Sadie is just fine."

"You don't know that for sure."

"That's true, I don't," Dad admitted. "But when I don't know things, I look to similar experiences in the past. In the past, every time we haven't known where Grandma was, she turned out to be just fine. So this time, I'm sure it will end up the same way. Don't you think so?"

I wanted to think so. But I knew something Dad didn't: MaLa, whoever they were, had kidnapped Grandma.

Well, since Grandma was a grown-up, she couldn't exactly be *kid*napped. But she'd been *grown-up*-napped!

"Come on, Pipe," Dad said. "Let's get you back to bed."

I scooped up the blob version of Cosmo and followed Dad down the hall to my room. He kissed me goodnight again. "Go to sleep, take two," he said.

But take two of sleep didn't work, either. Now I had two problems.

1. Grandma Sadie was still missing.
2. MaLa told me to bury the space dust, but I didn't have it anymore. All of the space dust was in Cosmo!

Now that Dad had left the room, Cosmo was alive again. He snuggled close, gurgling his good Cosmo gurgles.

"I don't know how the space dust brought you to life, but I'm so glad it did," I told him. "I've known you for only a day, but now I can't imagine my life without you."

He gurgled some more.

"But now I don't have any space dust left for MaLa," I said. "I don't know what to do. Unless..."

Cosmo looked up at me, waiting for the *unless*.

"Cosmo!" I said. "Remember how I told you I wasn't excited to get space dust at first, because space dust looks just like regular dust?"

He nodded.

"Good job nodding," I said. "And listen to this: Maybe I can give regular dust to MaLa and they won't know the difference. They'll let Grandma go, and everything will get back to normal!

Can you turn on your light again?"

Cosmo blinked and began to glow. "Thanks, boy," I said, and I jumped out of bed. For the first time in my life, I was excited about cleaning. Well, I was excited about dusting.

I swiped a finger across my shelf and got a good chunk of dust. Now I just needed the bottle to put it in.

The bottle...where had I put it?

Oh! That's right. I'd hidden it in my top desk drawer. I pulled the drawer open and grabbed the bottle. I unscrewed the top and smushed the dust inside.

"That looks like enough dust, right, Cosmo?" I asked.

Cosmo shook his head.

"Hmm. Maybe I *should* put some more dust in there, just in case."

I swiped my finger across the next shelf, but my finger came up dustless.

Where could I find more dust? I gazed around the room, not seeing any, until my eyes fell on the top of my bulletin board. There was a layer of dust along the edge of the frame. I climbed up on my desk chair, which I'm not allowed to do. Then I stood on my desk, which I'm *also* not allowed to do. If Mom or Dad saw me, they'd really be mad.

But Mom and Dad were all the way down the hall. I swiped my finger across the top of the bulletin board and put the dust in the bottle.

Then I put the top back on the bottle and climbed down off my desk.

"Phew, Cosmo," I said. "That should be enough for MaLa. Now all I have to do is bury the bottle in the window box. Let's do it right now, okay?"

He nodded.

I opened my window and shivered. The night air was really chilly. Luckily, this wouldn't take long. I scooped out some dirt next to the irises. (There was an artist named Georgia O'Keeffe who was famous for painting flowers. Her purple iris paintings are my favorites, and that's why Dad planted irises in my window box.) I put the bottle of dust in the hole and smoothed the dirt back into place, being extra careful around the roots of my flowers. Then I patted down the dirt. My fingers were cold. I was ready to close the window and get back under my cozy covers with Cosmo.

But before I did that, I looked up at the night sky. Grandma had told me that when we look up at the night sky, we're just seeing a sliver of the stars in our galaxy—the Milky Way galaxy. There are billions of stars in the Milky Way, and billions more galaxies in the universe. No matter how many space trips Grandma took, she'd never get to see it all.

"I'm going to get you back, Grandma,"
I said to the sky. "I promise you."

Another Email

My plan was to stay awake all night long. That way, when MaLa came to collect the space dust, I'd get to see who they were and make sure they let Grandma go.

But when I opened my eyes, it was morning. I didn't even remember closing my eyes. The sun was streaming through the blinds. The sun reminded me of Grandma, too. She'd told me a bunch of facts about it, such as:

1. The sun is a star.
2. It's not the brightest star in our galaxy, the Milky Way. But it's the closest to Earth. That's why it seems to be the brightest star in the sky.
3. The sun is actually not close at all. It would take us months and months in our fastest spacecraft to get there.

Cosmo was sleeping next to me. The light from the sun was making his cute purple cheeks a little bit rosy. I climbed out of bed, careful not to wake him, and opened the window to check if MaLa had come. The dirt in the window box was all messed up, and the irises were flopping

sideways. It didn't look at all like a Georgia O'Keeffe painting. But I didn't care. I rooted my hand around to check that the bottle was gone—and it was!

"Cosmo, wake up!"

He opened his eyes and made his morning gurgle sounds.

"The bottle's gone!" I said. "C'mon. Let's see if Grandma's back. We can fix the flowers later."

I picked up Cosmo and ran down the hall. Mom and Dad were sitting at the kitchen table, drinking coffee.

"Good morning, sweetheart," Mom said. "I heard you had a hard time falling asleep last night."

"I was worried about Grandma," I said. "Did she call yet?"

"Not yet," Mom said.

"Maybe she emailed," I said.

"I already checked my email."

"You should check again," I told her.

Mom picked up her cell phone. "I've been checking all morning," she said.

"I'm sure that Grandma Sadie is FINE," Dad said.

"I should get a cell phone so I can check my emails all the time, just like you," I told Mom.

"No, I don't think so," Mom said. "Eight years old is too young for a cell phone. But nice try."

"You can use my computer to check now, if you want," Dad said. "But you have to leave your slime here."

I didn't want to be away from Cosmo.

But he'd turned back into a blob anyway, since Mom and Dad were in the room. And I'd be gone for just a few minutes.

"You'll be fine here," I whispered, and I put Cosmo-the-blob on my chair. Then I headed to Dad's office. I logged into my email. There was one new message. My heart felt like it had leapt up into my throat.

Please let it be from Grandma. Please. PLEASE!

But the sender was MaLa, and the message said:

Dear Piper Maclane,

This email will disappear within five minutes of being opened.

We know that you tried to trick us into thinking Earth dust was space dust. But we cannot be tricked. We will get our hands on the space dust, no matter what we have to do to get it.

Do not tell anyone about this email.

Sincerely,

MaLa

I stared at the computer screen.

I didn't know what to do. What could I do?

Well...I could write back to MaLa and explain that the space dust had spilled onto Cosmo. But what if they said I had to put *Cosmo* in the window box?

"Anything?" Dad asked from the doorway.

"What do you mean?"

"Is there an email from your grandma?"

"Oh," I said. "No, there's not."

Dad stepped forward. My heart thumped with worry that he'd see what MaLa had written, but the message disappeared before he got close enough to see the screen.

Dad put his hand on my shoulder.

"I know it's hard to be worried about someone you love."

"Yeah, it is."

"Your mom is having a tough time, too," he said. "To tell you the truth, so am I. I have an idea— let's all do a family project together."

Family Project

"What kind of family project?" I asked.

"We've been talking about cleaning out the basement for a year or so," Dad said. "Today could be the day to do it."

"Cleaning out the basement is definitely not going to make me feel better about Grandma being missing," I said.

"It'll be a good distraction from worrying about her," Dad said.

"Ugh," I said. "I've done so much cleaning in the last couple of days. The other night, I had to clean my room after I made slime. Then after school yesterday, Claire and I had to clean the third-grade classrooms with Mr. Leon, and last night I dusted—"

Oops. Didn't mean to tell him that.

"You dusted?" Dad asked.

"I saw a little dust and I wiped

it up, that's all," I said.

"I'm sure there's tons of dust in the basement," Dad said. "Let's go."

I didn't have much choice, so I followed him downstairs. Mom came, too. So did Cosmo...but only because I carried him. There were lots of boxes of old stuff to go through. Mom said we should separate things into two piles.

Pile number 1: Things to keep

Pile number 2: Things to get rid of

I picked a box near the door. Dad sat next to me with a box of his own, and we each started sorting things. Mom's old law school papers went into pile number 2. My old art supplies went into pile number 1. Pretty soon the box was empty.

I was about to set it aside and start on my second box when I had a thought: If I decorated this empty box, I could make it into something for Cosmo. Just like dogs get to have doghouses, Cosmo could have a place of his own!

Good thing I had my old art supplies down there, because I was able to get to work right away.

I thought about what I should draw. What would make Cosmo feel at home?

Since Grandma got the dust from space, I decided I'd draw some constellations. Did you know that there are eighty-eight constellations? That's something Grandma told me. Another thing she told me is that the outlines of constellations can change over time as stars move through their orbits in space.

I drew my three favorite constellations.

1. Ursa Major, which is a big bear
2. Ursa Minor, which is a small bear
3. Leo, which is a lion

When I was done, I cut out a little door so it would be easier for Cosmo to crawl inside. Then I grabbed an old T-shirt Dad had put in pile number 2.

"Hey, whatcha doing with that?" he asked.

"If you're going to throw it away, can I keep it?"

"What for?"

"I'm making a little clubhouse for my slime," I said. "If I fold up a T-shirt and put it in the bottom of the box, it'll be much cozier."

"A cozy clubhouse for your *slime*?" Dad asked.

"Uh huh."

"You're a funny girl, Piper," he said.

"So can I have the shirt?"

"Sure," he said.

"Thanks," I said.

I put the T-shirt in. Then I lifted Cosmo up and put him on top of it. "Do you like it?" I whispered to him, so Dad wouldn't hear.

Cosmo didn't answer. He was just a blob right then.

"Don't worry," I told him. "You don't have to stay in here all the time. Just whenever you want."

"Oh!" Mom called out.

Dad and I scrambled up and ran over

to her. She was holding an old photo.

"Look, Piper," she said. "It's Grandma Sadie when she was eight years old, just like you."

"Wow," I said. I took the picture from her so I could look closer. Grandma had long hair in braids with a paintbrush tucked behind one ear and was wearing a checkered dress. I couldn't tell the colors because the photo was black and white. "She was so cute."

"Cutest thing in the world," Mom said. "Except for you."

And Cosmo, I thought.

I stared at the picture for a few more seconds before handing it back to Mom. "This goes in pile number 1, for saving," I told her.

"Of course," she said.

I went back to check on Cosmo. "Are you enjoying your slime clubhouse?" I asked softly.

But when I peeked inside the box, Cosmo was gone!

6

Who Could It Be?

"Oh no!" I cried.

Mom and Dad rushed over. "What's wrong?" Mom asked.

"Co...I mean, my slime. It's missing!"

"Maybe you left it upstairs," Mom said.

"No, I had it down here, I'm sure of it," I said. "I made a cozy slime clubhouse out of an old box, and I put my slime inside. Then you found Grandma's picture, so I went to look at it. Now my slime is gone!"

"I'm sorry, Pipe," Mom said. "Maybe we can bend the no-making-slime-for-a-week rule and make a new batch."

"I don't want a new batch," I said. "I just want Co...I want *this one!*"

Mom patted my back.

"Hey, would you look at that," Dad said, and he pointed to the space in between the slats of the basement stairs. "Isn't that your slime down there?"

64

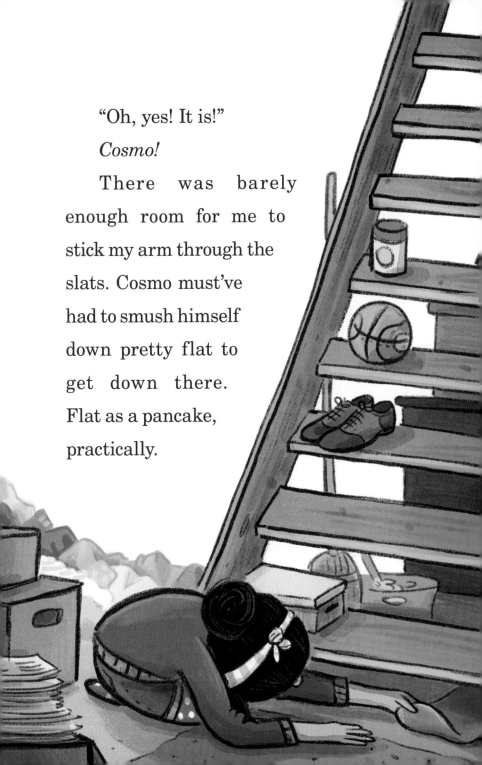

"Oh, yes! It is!"

Cosmo!

There was barely enough room for me to stick my arm through the slats. Cosmo must've had to smush himself down pretty flat to get down there. Flat as a pancake, practically.

But I guess slime can do that kind of thing. When I pulled him back up, he didn't look much like the slime pet I'd made. I hoped he'd be okay when he turned alive again. I tried to round him out a bit.

Then the doorbell rang. "Are you expecting anyone?" Dad asked.

Mom and I shook our heads.

"I don't want to get my hopes up thinking it could be..." Mom's voice trailed off.

"Who?" I asked. "Who could it be?"

"Maybe Grandma," Dad said.

Or maybe MaLa, I thought.

The three of us raced up the stairs. I had Cosmo-the-flattened-blob in my arms. "We're coming!" I shouted, and I opened the door.

Two Visitors

It wasn't Grandma on the other side of the door. And it wasn't MaLa, either. It was Claire.

"Oh, hi," I said. "It's you."

"Most people are happy when I come over," Claire said. "But you don't seem happy at all."

"I *am* happy," I told her. "I just thought you might be someone else, that's all. What are you doing here?"

"We're friends now," she said. "So I came to play with you...and YKW."

"Huh?"

She glanced at my parents, then lowered her voice. *"You know who,"* she said.

Oh. She meant Cosmo.

"I rang the doorbell at least five times," Claire went on. "I saw your parents' cars in the driveway, so I knew you were home. What took you so long?"

"We were cleaning the basement," I said. "We didn't hear the doorbell down there. I guess..."

"You guess what?" Claire asked.

I shook my head. I couldn't answer her with Mom and Dad right there. But I'd figured something out. When Dad and I had gone to the back of the basement to see the picture Mom had found, I'd left Cosmo by himself near the stairs. He must've heard the doorbell. I bet he was trying to go upstairs and answer it, and that's when he fell in between the stair slats.

"Can I play with Claire now?" I asked Mom and Dad.

"And miss out on our fun family cleaning project?" Dad asked.

I was pretty sure he was kidding. But even so, Claire, the most popular girl in my class, was standing right there. Why did he have to make such silly jokes in front of her?

"Mom, can I?" I asked.

"Sure you can," she said.

"Let's play outside," Claire said. "I want to show you the twisty trick I can do on my scooter."

"Stay near the house," Dad said.

"We will," I promised.

As soon as the front door closed and Mom and Dad were out of sight, Cosmo turned alive again. I felt his body getting softer in my arms.

I mean, slime is already soft. But there's the softness of regular blob slime and the softness of alive slime. I don't know exactly how to explain the difference, but it's probably like holding a real live kitten instead of a stuffed animal kitten.

His shape started to go back to normal. His body rounded out, and he blinked his eyes open.

"I'm so glad you're okay!" I told him.

"Can I hold him?" Claire asked.

"Uh…" I didn't want to let go of him just yet, but it's hard to say no to Claire. "Okay."

I handed Cosmo over, and Claire squeezed him close. "Oh, you're so cute. You're *soooooooo* cute."

Cosmo gurgled at her. He seemed really happy. I knew I should be happy that he was happy, but I felt...

Well, if you want to know the truth, I felt jealous. *I* wanted to be the one holding Cosmo and making him that happy.

"Don't you want to show me your twisty trick?" I asked.

"Oh, yeah," Claire said.

"I better take Cosmo, then," I said. "It might be too dangerous for him to do it with you."

I wasn't trying to be mean. It's just that Cosmo is *my* pet, which means it's *my* job to protect him.

Cosmo and I sat on the porch steps

74

to watch. Claire put on her helmet. She scooted down the walkway to the sidewalk right in front of our house. Then she kicked off the back and made the scooter go around and around. Cosmo clapped his teeny little purple slime hands, and I clapped my regular hands.

Claire scooted back up the walkway.

"That was so cool," I said. "Right, Cosmo?"

But when I turned to him, he was back to being a slime blob. Just then, a car pulled up in front of the house, and a woman got out. She had red hair that was cut into a triangle shape. I'd never seen anyone with that haircut before.

"Are you Piper Maclane?" she asked.

I was about to say yes, but before I could, Claire asked, "Who wants to know?"

That was probably a good question to ask, since this woman was a stranger, and you're not supposed to tell strangers your name. Actually, you're not supposed to talk to them at all.

But I knew it might be MaLa coming to tell me something about Grandma, so I said, "*I'm* Piper Maclane."

"Special delivery," the woman said. She handed me an envelope. "This is just for your eyes, not your friend's."

"Okay," I said.

The woman got back into her car and drove away. I ripped open the envelope. There was a letter inside. I twisted around so Claire wouldn't see.

Dear Piper Maclane,

You didn't take our email seriously, so we're trying home delivery. Bury the REAL space dust in the window box outside your bedroom by sunrise tomorrow—or else you'll NEVER see your grandma again!

Do not talk to anyone about this letter.

Sincerely,
MaLa

How to Not Tell a Secret

"**What does the letter say?**" Claire asked.

"I can't tell you," I said. "It's a secret."

"You didn't even know the woman who gave it to you," Claire said. "How can you have a secret with her?"

"The letter says not to talk to anyone

about it," I said. "That makes it a secret."

Claire folded her arms across her chest. "You should still tell me, even if it is a secret, because I'm good at keeping them. I haven't told anyone about Cosmo."

"This is an even bigger secret," I said. "Someone's *life* is at stake."

Claire's eyes widened. "Whose life?"

"I can't tell you."

"Ugh, I knew you were going to say that," she said. "But what if you tell me without actually telling me?"

"How could I do that?" I asked.

"We could play charades."

"I don't know what that is," I said.

"It's a game where one person acts out something, and the other person tries to guess what they're saying," Claire explained.

"It'd take too long, and I don't have a lot of time. I have things I have to do *right now*."

"What things?"

That was the problem. I didn't know what I could do to get Grandma back— besides give up Cosmo, which I didn't want to do. I just *couldn't*. So I needed some time to think about other options that would keep *everybody* safe.

"You should go home now," I told Claire. I picked up Cosmo and moved toward the front door.

"Wait!" Claire called out. "Whatever it is that you don't want to say, you could write it down."

"No, I—"

Claire cut me off. "The letter said not to *talk* to anyone about it," she said. "Writing is not the same thing as talking."

"Well, that's true," I said.

"Get some paper and a pen right now!" Claire said.

"I'll write it in the dirt," I said. "That way I can scratch out the words as soon as you're done reading them. It'll be like an email that disappears."

"What kind of email just disappears?" Claire asked.

"It's not important," I said. "I need to find a good scratching stick."

We hunted around the front yard. Cosmo helped, too. "Here's one!" Claire said. She hovered over my shoulder as I wrote.

Seeing that sentence written out made it seem even scarier. My heart started to pound. Poor Grandma Sadie—kidnapped!

Someone named MaLa kidnapped my grandma

Claire read it out loud: "Someone named MaLa kidnapped my grandma."

"Shhh," I said, and I scratched out the words until they disappeared.

"That's weird," Claire said.

"Actually, it's horrible," I said.

"Horrible, but mostly weird."

"Why?" I asked.

"Because MaLa is the name of the company where my Uncle Ricky works."

Hop On

"**MaLa is the name of your**
Uncle Ricky's company?" I asked.

"Well, it's not *his* company," Claire
said. "He doesn't own it. He just works
there. He's a scientist."

"And it's spelled that same way?" I asked. "Capital M, lowercase a, capital L, and lowercase a?"

"Yup," Claire said. "It's an abbreviation, short for Magna Labs. Everyone who works there calls it MaLa."

"Cosmo, do you know what this means?" I asked.

Cosmo shook his head.

"OMG!" Claire said. "He shook his head! That's amazing! Don't you think that's amazing?"

"Yes," I agreed. "But the thing that matters most is saving my grandma. No offense, Cosmo."

Cosmo did not look offended. He gurgled, which I think meant, "That's okay."

"Do you know the address for MaLa?" I asked Claire.

"321 Quantum Road," she said. "I heard my dad talking about what a weird place it is, and the address got stuck in my head."

"Okay, let's go."

"Hang on," Claire said. "Why don't we just call my uncle?" She pulled a cell phone out of her pocket.

My eyes almost bugged out of my head. "You have a cell phone?" I asked, feeling jealous of Claire all over again.

"My mom said eight years old is too young to get one," I said.

"Well, I'm eight and a *half*," Claire said. "And Uncle Ricky's number is saved in here." She pressed a button and held the phone to her ear.

"NO!" I shouted. "Hang up! Hang up right now!"

"Okay, okay," Claire said, and she pressed a button on the screen. "But why?"

"Your uncle might be the one who kidnapped my grandma."

"Uncle Ricky would never kidnap anyone," Claire said. "Take that back right now."

I put the hand that wasn't holding Cosmo on my hip. "I can't take it back without seeing for myself," I said.

"We don't even know for sure that it's

the right place," Claire said. "There could be lots of companies with the name MaLa. Or it could be a person. You thought it was a person at first, didn't you?"

"Yeah, but I knew it was a weird name for a person," I said. "It's got to be your uncle's company."

"Like I said, it's not *his* company," Claire said.

"Fine. Either way, we've got to go there right now," I said. "Except... oh no!"

"What?"

"It's *Saturday*," I said. "Companies are closed on Saturdays. If no one is at MaLa, how can we save Grandma?"

"MaLa is open on Saturdays," Claire said.

"It is?"

"Yeah, my uncle always says that if you're in the middle of a science experiment, you can't stop working just because it's the weekend."

"Oh, phew."

"But the real problem is that MaLa is all the way across town," Claire said. "It's too far to walk."

"We can take your scooter."

"I've never scooted that far before," Claire said.

"Please," I said. "Even if your uncle didn't take Grandma—"

"He didn't," Claire said.

"Even so, that's where she is," I said. "I'm sure of it."

"Are you going to bring Cosmo?" Claire asked.

"Of course."

"Okay." Claire stepped onto her scooter. "Hop on the back."

"Wait a sec," I said. I picked up the good scratching stick and wrote a note to Mom and Dad in the dirt.

They'd probably still be mad that I left the front lawn when they had told me to stay close. But at least they wouldn't be worried.

"Okay," I told Claire. "I'm almost ready to go."

Scoot

Before I could go anywhere, I had to run inside to grab my bike helmet. It wouldn't be safe to scoot without it.

Cosmo needed a helmet, too. I took Dad's off the hook. When I put it on Cosmo, it was practically the size of his whole body. "You'll be extra safe now," I told him.

"Piper, is that you?" Dad shouted up from the basement.

"Yeah!" I shouted back. "I had to get something, but now I'm going back outside to play with Claire some more."

"Have fun!" Dad called.

"Love you!" Mom added.

"Love you guys, too," I said.

I felt a teensy bit guilty that I was

going somewhere without telling them.

Okay, more than a teensy bit.

But they'd be so happy when I rescued Grandma, and that was all that mattered.

Cosmo and I headed outside. I put him on my shoulder. Claire held on to the handlebars of her scooter. I held on to Claire with one arm and Cosmo with the other. He stuck his little arms out from Dad's helmet and held on to me.

Claire kicked off the ground on the right side, and I kicked off on the left. We scooted down the street and around the corner.

At first it felt like regular scooting. We passed by people walking on the sidewalk. Since they were walking and we were scooting, it was normal for us to move faster than they were.

But then I noticed that we were passing people on bikes and rollerblades, too. And pretty soon, we were also passing moving cars. They were just shapes that we whooshed past.

WHOOSH!

WHOOSH!

WHOOSH!

Everything all around us was a blur—the people, the cars, the street signs, the buildings. That's how fast we were going. I stopped kicking on my side of the scooter, but we just kept going faster and faster.

"Hey, Claire!" I shouted. The wind was so loud in my ears that I could hardly hear myself. "You don't have to kick so fast!"

"I'm not kicking at all!" Claire shouted back. "I thought YOU were doing all the kicking!"

"No!" I said. "I stopped kicking awhile ago!"

"Then how—"

I looked at Cosmo and saw how. "Oh!" I said. "It's Cosmo! He was the brightest lightbulb last night, and today he's the fastest jet engine!"

"What do you mean?"

"He has superpowers!" I said.

"He's alive?" Claire asked. "But I thought he'd turn into a blob again, with all these people walking and driving around us."

"They look blurry to us," I said. "Which means we must look blurry to them. I guess Cosmo can stay alive in front of other people if he's just a blur."

"Oh, cool!" Claire said. "Wheeeeeeeeeeeeeeeeeeeeee!"

"Wheeeeeeeeeeeeeeeeeeee!" I shouted back.

Cosmo made the scooter go even *faster*. We whipped down the last couple of streets, and in no time at all, we were in front of 321 Quantum Road. Claire and I pulled off our helmets. I helped Cosmo take his off, too.

There weren't any people nearby. It was just the three of us, staring at an office building. It was big and gray and plain. I bet if Keith Haring were alive, he'd want to paint a mural across the front. (Keith Haring was an artist who was famous for his colorful murals. He made lots of plain spaces much more interesting.)

But Keith Haring wasn't there. And

Claire and I were on a mission that didn't have anything to do with murals.

The building had a plain, gray door with a sign on it that read:

I took some deep breaths to get ready to ring the bell. But before I could, Claire reached out and rang it herself.

A few seconds later, the door swung open and a man in a dark suit looked down at us. "State your business," he said to Claire and me. (Cosmo had turned back into a blob, of course.)

"Well, we don't exactly have any *business*," Claire said. "But we—"

"Authorized personnel only," the man interrupted.

"I don't know what that means," I said.

"It means you can't come in," he said. "Run along now."

"But my grandma—" I started to say, at the same time that Claire said, "But my uncle—"

The man didn't wait to hear the ends of our sentences. He slammed the door shut, and I heard him turn the lock on the other side. I pulled on the handle anyway.

The door didn't budge. We were locked out.

Hello,
Uncle Ricky

Claire and I looked at each other.

"Now we should call my uncle, right?" she said.

"Yeah, okay," I said.

"Great!" She whipped her cell phone out of her pocket. "He's a really nice guy.

Everyone who meets him says that. He'd never kidnap your grandma. He'd never kidnap *anyone*. You'll see."

She pressed some buttons and held the phone to her ear. I stood right next to her and leaned my head against hers so I could hear whatever her uncle had to say.

The only sound was the phone ringing. *Brrrrrring...brrrrrring.*

"When he answers, I'm going to do the talking," Claire said. "He's MY uncle, after all."

"He hasn't even answered the phone," I said.

Brrrrrring...brrrr—

"Hello?" a man's voice said.

"Hello, Uncle Ricky?" Claire said.

"Claire, is that you?"

"Yes. And you'll never guess where I am."

"Where?"

"Here!" Claire said.

"Here?" Uncle Ricky asked. "I don't understand."

"I'm right outside the front door at Magna Labs," she told him. "I came with my friend Piper, because, well...Piper thinks her grandma might be in the building somewhere."

"I got a letter, that's why," I blurted out. "Plus two emails. Grandma Sadie

was kidnapped! You'd better not have done anything to hurt her, or I'll—"

"Cool it, Piper," Claire said. "I told you Uncle Ricky didn't have anything to do with it. Besides, I get to do the talking, remember?"

"Fine," I said.

"So, Uncle Ricky," Claire continued. "We came down here to rescue Piper's grandma. We rang the bell like the sign says, and the man who answered the door was very rude. You should tell your boss and get him in trouble."

"But first let us in, so we can find my grandma," I said.

"Yeah, first that. Okay?" Claire said.

"No, not okay," Uncle Ricky said.

"Huh?" Claire said.

"I'm not going to let the two of you in," he said. "You shouldn't be here at all."

"But—" I started.

"And another thing," Claire's Uncle Ricky interrupted. "What happens in Cell 8 is none of your concern. You hear me? Cell 8 does not concern you!"

There was a click on the other end of the line. Claire's uncle had hung up.

Flatter Than
a Pancake

Claire dropped the phone from her ear. Her face was red and her eyes were shiny.

"Are you going to cry?" I asked.

"What? No, of course not," Claire said. "I never cry. I just get mad."

"Well, I cry sometimes," I said. I could feel tears building up behind my eyeballs. I blinked a hundred times superfast to make them go away. But it wasn't working. I was too worried about Grandma, and a few big fat tears spilled out of my eyes.

Cosmo gurgled worriedly. "It's okay, boy, it's okay," I said, wiping my eyes. Even though it was NOT okay. Not at all.

"Now what?" Claire asked.

"I don't know," I told her. "We're right back where we started."

"Well, not exactly," she said. "We started at your house, and now we're here, at MaLa. And there's something else, too."

"What's that?" I asked.

"Uncle Ricky said that what happens in Cell 8 is none of our business. Cell 8. I bet that's where they're keeping your grandma."

"That's probably true," I said. "But what good does that do us? We can't get through a locked door."

"Too bad we don't know any ghosts," Claire said. "In the movies, ghosts can pass through locked doors. If we had a ghost friend, they could pass through the door and unlock it for us."

"Ghosts aren't real," I told her. "There's nothing that could pass through this door. Except..."

"Except what?"

"Cosmo!" I said.

"Cosmo can pass through a door?" Claire asked.

"No, but he might be able to squish down under it. He's slime, after all." I looked at Cosmo. "What do you think, boy? Can you do it?"

He nodded his head.

"Okay, let's try it."

I set Cosmo down at my feet. There was a teensy tiny space between the ground and the door—even smaller than the space between the slats of my basement stairs. It seemed way too small for Cosmo to fit. My breath was caught in my throat.

Cosmo made himself flat as a pancake again. But a pancake was too thick. He went even flatter. Flat as a crepe, which is a really, really thin pancake. In seconds, he disappeared under the door completely.

"What if there's someone waiting on the other side of the door?" Claire said. "Then he won't be able to come alive and unlock it."

"Oh no, I didn't think about that!" I cried. "What if they scoop him up and kidnap him, just like they kidnapped my grandma?"

Claire patted me on the back. "I don't know what to say."

"There's nothing to say," I told her.

"There's...wait, did you hear that?" she asked.

"Hear what?"

But then I heard it. It sounded like the lock on the other side of the door was being turned.

"Try it," Claire whispered.

I pushed down on the handle, and the door opened!

321 Quantum Road

On the other side of the door, Cosmo was waiting for us.

He looked just like his round, adorable self again. It was hard to believe that he'd been flatter than a pancake just a minute ago. He reached his little arms up toward me. I grabbed him and held him close.

"You're a very good boy, Cosmo," I said.

He gurgled happily.

We looked down the long, dimly lit hallway. In the distance, I heard footsteps coming from the left. "We'd better go," Claire said.

"This way," I said, leading her to the right. We moved very quietly, but very quickly, turning down another hallway and past a bunch of science labs. You could tell they were labs because each door had a sign on it. They were numbered, but I couldn't tell how many there were. They seemed to go on and on and on.

And on and on.

Some of the labs were empty, but some had people in them. Claire picked up her scooter, and we tiptoed past those rooms.

"Everything says lab, not cell," I said.

"Maybe my uncle meant Lab 8?"

But we passed Lab 8, and no one was in there—no scientists, and no Grandma, either.

We kept going. But I guess we weren't quiet enough. As we passed the doorway to Lab 12, I heard a man's voice say, "Hey, I think there are a couple of kids out in the hall."

"No, there couldn't be," another man answered.

Claire gasped. "That's Uncle Ricky," she whispered.

"I'm glad he doesn't know we're in

here, or he'd come kick us out for sure!"
I whispered back.

"Did you say kids?" a woman asked.
Her voice was familiar. But who was she?

It didn't matter. Claire, Cosmo, and
I walked faster down the hall.
We were practically running. Behind
us the woman shouted, "It's you! I
knew it!"

I snuck a look over my shoulder.
"It's triangle-hair lady!" I told Claire.

"Plus Uncle Ricky," she said.
"And more people, too!"

"We've gotta get out of here!"

Cosmo was just a blob now, with
everyone looking. Claire placed her

scooter on the floor. "Hop on, we'll go faster," she said.

I jumped on the back, hanging

on to Claire with one arm and Cosmo with the other. But we weren't going nearly as fast as before. Triangle-hair lady and the other scientists were on our tails.

"I've almost got 'em," Uncle Ricky shouted.

I felt his fingertips scraping at the back of my shirt. "Faster!" I told Claire.

"I'm trying!" she said.

We turned a corner. For an instant, we were out of sight, and that instant was all it took. Cosmo came alive, and the scooter took off like a race car. In a flash, we were at the end of the second hallway and turning onto another.

"Good boy, Cosmo!" I said.

Doors were whipping past us. Everything was a blur. I couldn't tell if we were passing more labs or if one of the rooms might be Cell 8. I thought I saw a room full of ducks.

Ducks?!

That didn't make any sense. This was a building, not a pond.

"Cosmo, you're going to have to slow down," I said. "We need to be able to look for Grandma Sadie."

But he didn't slow down. Instead, we headed toward—oh no! A stairwell!

Going down the stairs on a scooter was going to be a disaster!

The scooter shot forward. I squeezed my eyes shut and hung on to Claire, waiting for the crash landing.

But we didn't crash. Instead, we bounced down and down more stairwells. At the very bottom, Cosmo slowed the scooter to a regular pace.

"Whew," Claire whispered. "I didn't know if we were going to make it."

"Good boy for keeping us safe," I told Cosmo. I stepped off the back of the scooter so I could walk a little. My legs felt super wobbly.

"Is this the basement?" Claire asked.

Cosmo nodded.

"Do you think they keep prisoners down here?" she asked.

"There's only one way to find out," I said, and I took a step forward on my wobbly legs.

Out of Here

We walked down two deserted hallways that didn't have any rooms that looked like prison cells. When we turned the corner to the third hallway, though, I saw a closed door that was padlocked on the outside. At the top was a tiny window with bars in it, just like a window in a jail cell. A sign next to the door read Cell 1.

"If that's Cell 1, then Cell 8 must be—" Claire said.

"Down there," I said. "Let's go!"

We raced past the doors—odd numbers on the right, even numbers on the left. Seconds later, I was standing in front of a locked door marked Cell 8. I jumped up to try to see through the bars at the top.

"Grandma?" I cried.

"Pipsqueak, is that you?" she answered back.

"It's me!" I said. "It's so good to hear your voice!"

"Yours too!"

"My friend Claire is with me," I said. "And also...another friend. Wait till you see him. Well, you might not be able to see him. I'll explain everything, just as soon as we break into your cell."

I pulled at the padlock.

"What's your plan to break in?" Claire asked.

"I don't have one yet," I said.

I looked around to see if there were any tools I could use to break into Grandma's cell.

"Maybe I can smash the lock with your scooter," I told Claire.

"But what if you break it?" she asked.

"That's the point."

"Not the lock," she said. "My scooter."

"My grandma is more important than your scooter."

Claire was quiet for a few seconds. Cosmo reached for the lock and gurgled.

"You see, Cosmo thinks breaking the lock is more important than your scooter, too," I told Claire.

"I suppose you're right," she said. She pushed the handlebars toward me. "Here. I'll hold Cosmo while you do the smashing."

Cosmo reached for the lock and gurgled again, louder this time.

"I know you want to help, boy," I told him. "But the door is locked on this side, not the other side. If you slipped under the door, you wouldn't be able to do anything."

I handed him to Claire. Cosmo stuck out an arm and swiped at the padlock.

"Stand back," I told her. "I don't want to hurt you guys."

"I can't," Claire said. "Cosmo won't let go."

"C'mon, Cosmo," I said. "We've gotta break the lock and get Grandma out before those scientists find us down here."

I pulled on his arm. I didn't want to hurt him, but I had to get him to let go.

Except he wouldn't. His hand was...well, it was stuck inside the padlock, right where you'd insert a key.

Cosmo's face was twisted in concentration. Then there was a *pop* sound. The padlock slid open and tumbled to the floor. The door swung open.

"Grandma!"

"Pipsqueak!"

I jumped toward her and gave her the biggest hug in the history of hugs. She had a bit of dirt smudged on her cheek, and it looked like she hadn't brushed her hair in a while. "Oh, I'm so happy to see you," I said.

"Not as happy as I am to see you," she said. "I missed your face so much. I missed it even more than all the stars in the sky."

"It must've been so awful in here," I said. "Did you get any food or water?"

Grandma nodded. "There's a nice man named Eric who has been sneaking things in to me," she said.

"I can't believe anyone here is nice at all," Claire said. "I'm Claire, BTW."

"BTW means 'by the way,'" I told Grandma. "Claire is my friend from school. And that little blob she's holding is Cosmo. You can't tell he's alive, but—"

"Oh my," Grandma said, as Cosmo waved at her from Claire's arms.

"He's alive for you, too!" I said. "That makes three people he can stay alive for—me, Claire, and you!"

"You got the dust on him?" Grandma asked.

"Yeah," I said. "How did you know?"

"Eric told me space dust could have some amazing effects," Grandma said.

"The Eric who sneaked you the food down here?" I asked.

"Yes," she said. "I'll tell you everything, I promise. But first, we have to do a few things."

"Like get out of here?" Claire asked.

"You bet," Grandma said.

"The stairs are this way," I said.

The four of us headed down the hallway. I kept looking at Grandma. "I can't believe you're really real," I said.

"I can't believe Cosmo is really real," Grandma said.

"Me either," I said.

"Shh," Claire said.

"What?"

"I think I hear something."

We all stayed as quiet as we could, listening. The hallway was silent.

"I think we're okay," Grandma said.

We got to the end of the hallway and were just about to turn to the stairs when someone jumped out. "Aha!" he said.

"Oh no!" Claire cried. "Uncle Ricky!"

"Caught you!" he said.

My pet Slime

More to Explore

Bioluminescence

What do fireflies, some jellyfish, and Cosmo have in common?

If you said "they glow," you're right! Some creatures have the ability to give off light. This is called **bioluminescence** (BI-o-loo-muh-neh-sens).

Bioluminescence is a chemical reaction that's very common in the deep sea, where about three-fourths of creatures produce light. It's so dark in the deep, deep ocean that their light helps them find their way.

148

Bioluminescence can also lure prey, attract mates, or confuse predators. Sometimes, it provides camouflage that helps creatures avoid getting eaten.

Bioluminescent creatures include everything from some jellyfish, algae, and sharks to a few species of beetles and worms. (You might even guess that they glow by their names, like glowworms and lanternfish.)

While we don't know exactly why Cosmo glows, it's definitely a cool trick that comes in handy!

Constellations

When Piper wanted to make a cozy home for Cosmo, she decorated it with what she thought would make him feel at home: **constellations**.

Constellations are groups of stars that, when connected, form pictures in the sky. Many constellations date back thousands of years and represent animals, objects, or characters in mythology.

There are 88 constellations. Piper's favorites include Ursa Major (a big bear), Ursa Minor (a small bear), and Leo, which looks like a lion. On the next clear night, look up and see if you can find the Big Dipper, which is made up of seven bright stars and is part of Ursa Major. It's called the "Big Dipper" because, as you may have guessed, it looks like a giant spoon or ladle.

Constellations remind us that stories can be found everywhere, even in the stars. They're also fun to draw. Maybe you'll be inspired to create your own!

Piper MacLane's Glowing Slime Recipe

One thing that makes Cosmo so special is that he can glow in the dark. Here's how to make glowing slime at home (with your parents' help)! You'll need:

1. **A 6-ounce bottle of white or clear school glue**
2. **½ teaspoon baking soda**
3. **½ tablespoon glow powder (you can find this online)**
4. **1½ tablespoons contact lens solution that includes boric acid and sodium borate**

Squeeze all of the glue in a bowl. Next, slowly add the baking soda, which will make your slime more firm. (If you want stretchier slime, add a little water.) Add the glow powder, and mix it well. Finally, add the contact lens solution to "activate" your glowing slime!

(Note: If you can't find glow powder, you can also use glow-in-the-dark school glue or glow-in-the-dark craft paint, which most craft stores sell.)

About the Author

Courtney Sheinmel is a chocolate lover, a mac-and-cheese expert, and the author of over twenty highly celebrated books for kids and teens, including the middle grade series *The Kindness Club*, and the young readers' series *Stella Batts* and *Magic on the Map*. She lives in New York City.

About the Illustrator

Renée Kurilla has illustrated many books for kids. She lives just south of Boston with her husband, daughter, and a plump orange cat who springs to life the moment everyone else falls asleep. Renée loves drawing nature, animals, and projects that require a bit of research. When she is not drawing, she is likely to be found plucking at her ukulele or gluing together tiny dollhouse miniatures.

Don't miss Cosmo and Piper's next adventure

COMING SOON!

NOW AVAILABLE ON GETEPIC.COM

LOOK FOR THESE GREAT BOOKS FROM

VISIT THE WORLD'S LARGEST DIGITAL LIBRARY FOR KIDS AT

getepic.com